Michael Foreman

PANDA AND
THE BUSHFIRE

First American Edition
Copyright © 1986 by Michael Foreman

Published in the United States by
Prentice-Hall Books for Young Readers.
A Division of Simon and Schuster, Inc.
1230 Avenue of the Americas, New York, NY 10020

First published in Great Britain by
Hamish Hamilton Children's Books

10 9 8 7 6 5 4 3 2 1

Prentice-Hall Books for Young Readers is a
trademark of Simon and Schuster, Inc.

Library of Congress Cataloguing in Publication Data

Foreman, Michael, 1938–
   Panda and the bushfire.

Summary: with the help of Flying Lion, Panda
and his animal friends escape a fire in the Australian
bush and aid the firefighters in battling the blaze.
   [1. Fires—fiction,   2. Pandas—Fiction.
3. Animals—Fiction.   4. Australia—Fiction]   I. Title.
PZ7.F7583Pam 1986   [E]   86–4982
ISBN 0–13–648395–X

Printed in Italy

Michael Foreman

PANDA AND THE BUSHFIRE

Prentice-Hall Books for Young Readers

A Division of Simon and Schuster, Inc.
New York

The sun was setting beyond the sea. Panda and the winged lion sat on the
beach and watched the last light fade from the sky.

The first star appeared. 'Time to go,' said Panda, 'time to go home.'

Lion stretched his wings. 'All aboard,' he said, and Panda climbed onto his back. A little run and a jump and beating of wings, and the two friends were flying.

They followed the moon as it sailed upstream from the sea.

They flew all the starry night and in the morning left the sky to the sun, and rested in the cool of some trees.

Lion was soon asleep, but Panda lay and listened to the sounds all around him and felt the hot wind which was suddenly tugging at the tree tops.

The rustling sounds grew louder. Little creatures were scurrying through the grass and fallen leaves. Then larger creatures could be heard rushing through the scrub.

When a mob of kangaroos came booming out of the trees, even Lion woke up.
FIRE! The smell of smoke was unmistakable, and now a crackling dry roar
could also be heard.

Thump, thump, thump. Three furry bundles suddenly tumbled out of a tree and onto Panda and Lion.

'Scuse us,' gasped the biggest bundle and, picking up the smallest bundle, they set off as fast as they could scurry – which wasn't very fast.

The fire was approaching at a furious pace. Sparks carried by the wind
were falling all around and starting new fires. Now all of them were
surrounded by fires. The three furry bundles clung together and shivered
in the fierce heat. 'Quick!' shouted Panda, 'this way!' 'All aboard,' yelled Lion.

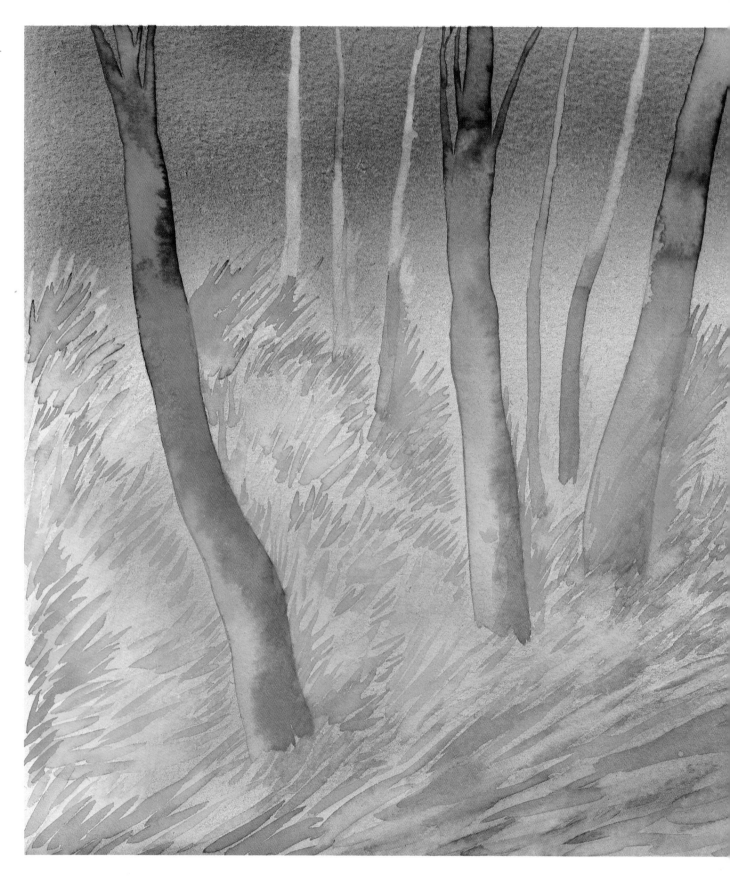

Panda helped the furry bundles onto Lion's back. Lion ran a few steps over the sparking scorching ground and beat his great wings up and down, up and down.

But the weight of his passengers was too great. He could not get off the
ground. He skidded to a halt, turned round and ran back the other way, as
fast as he could towards the rushing fire!

Again, Lion frantically beat his wings up and down, up and down, and this time the heat and the raging wind combined to lift Lion, Panda and the three furry bundles slowly off the ground.

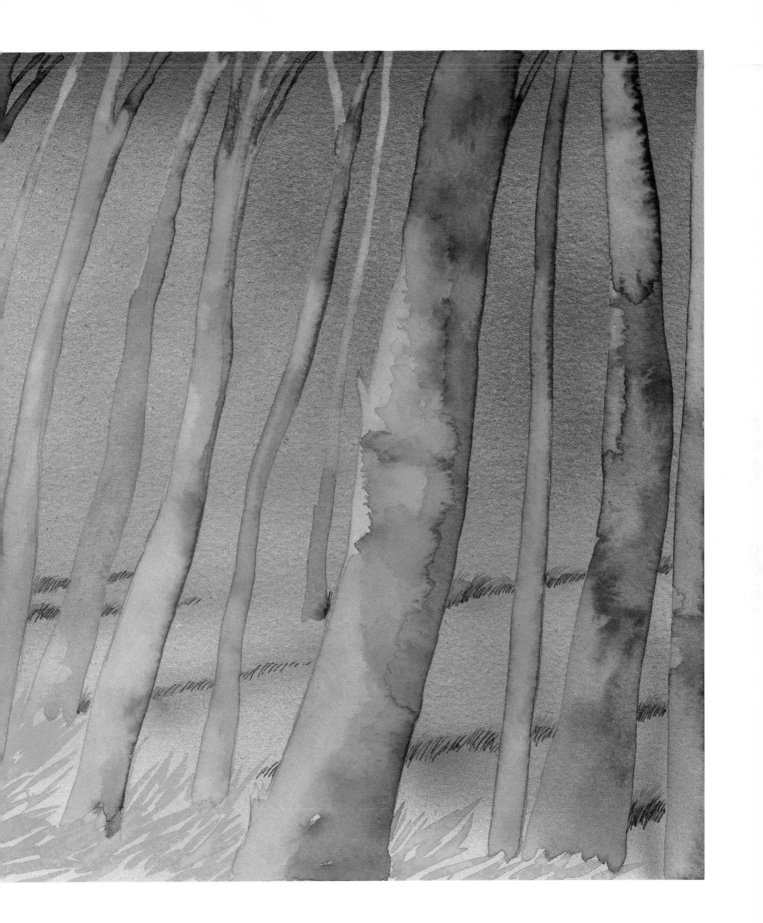

Flames leaped and licked at the straining lion. Panda, eyes streaming from the smoke, beat away the showers of sparks and blazing leaves.

Treetops exploded like giant fireworks all around them. Then, at last, they were above the flames.

Now they were tumbled about the black billowing sky in clouds of smoke, leaves and frightened birds.

'Hang on,' yelled Panda. 'Lion, I can see the river! Head for the river!'

As they flew over the river, they could see people on the far bank rushing
to beat out sparks carried on the wind.

Fire trucks were arriving. Hoses gushed and made rainbows

Exhausted, Lion made a skidding bellyflop on the wet bank. Panda and the
furry bundles rolled in all directions.

People were rushing about with buckets and hoses.

Panda and Lion took off again and helped by spraying the treetops. At last, the wind dropped and grew weaker and weaker, until it finally crept off in another direction.

A great cheer went up from the people. Panda and Lion were heroes. They had helped defeat the fire, and had saved the three koalas.

Late into the evening, over mugs of tea, Panda and Lion discussed the
adventures of the day.

Then they told the wide-eyed koalas and firefighters of other adventures,
and of their travels in distant lands.

That night, Panda and Lion stayed with the koalas in a treetop by the river.
The koalas told Panda that, one day, the burnt black trees on the other

bank would burst into new green leaves, and then all the creatures would
return to their old homes.

And Panda said that one day soon, he and Lion
must continue their long journey home.
And perhaps, just perhaps, the littlest koala,
who has fallen in love with flying,
will go with them.